Journeys
to Peace

Journeys to Peace

"A Parable of Love & Forgiveness"

TR BRENNAN

WESTBOW
PRESS®
A DIVISION OF THOMAS NELSON
& ZONDERVAN

WestBow Press books may be ordered through booksellers or by contacting:

WestBow Press
A Division of Thomas Nelson & Zondervan
1663 Liberty Drive
Bloomington, IN 47403
www.westbowpress.com
1 (866) 928-1240

ISBN: 978-1-9736-5643-2 (sc)
ISBN: 978-1-9736-5642-5 (hc)
ISBN: 978-1-9736-5644-9 (e)

Library of Congress Control Number: 2019902806

Print information available on the last page.

WestBow Press rev. date: 4/8/2019

This Book Is Dedicated To:

God the Father of Creation, His Son, Jesus Christ, and
the Holy Spirit.

First Nations people across the world who journeyed before us,
endured hardships and death brought on by hate and greed;
for that I am deeply sorry.

And to all people no matter race, color, or creed
who are hurt, lonely, depressed and fearful—may
you find the Way Maker, Jesus Christ, for
He will guide you through your journeys in life to peace.

A Special Thank You To:

Abba God, Yahshua, and Holy Spirit for inspiration,
wisdom, and guidance throughout this whole process.

Jamie, my husband who supports me always with
unconditional love and prayers.

Our daughter Jennifer, our miracle from God. Who brings never
ending laughter and joy into our lives, for this we are truly blessed.

To my parents who grew up in the depression, worked hard and
devoted their lives to providing better opportunities for their children.

To my cherished sister Heidi, who always supported me and
will forever be among the stars and in my heart.

To my beloved friend Sally, who encourages me in life as
we fellowship with tea and scripture.

To our dear friends, Barry and Luanne, who have taught us so much
about their Native culture and the love of Yah—Jesus Christ.

For answered prayers finding an awesome,
professional, Christian Editor:

Brittany Clarke
www.brittclarke.com

Contents

A Parable of Love

Dear children,

For those who are lonely, fearful, and in despair, may this parable of love lift your spirits, heal your soul, and bring a new hope to you.

May you be renewed with a desire to live life to the fullest and accomplish that which God the Father ordained for you.

You are His unique creation, and you are loved.

God's blessings and peace –

Chapter 1

The Cabin

I FONDLY REMEMBER MR. BOB CASTLEMAN. HE was a gentlemen's gentleman. He was a good man, a godly man. He cared about people and had a heart of grace like none other. His only purpose in life was to serve God and love His people—unbeknown to most. He accomplished this through his ministry, which was his life.

I met him long ago during a most difficult time in my life. I had everything but felt like I had nothing. I was alone, with no hope, no joy, and no desire to continue on living in the empty void people called life. It was Mr. Castleman who turned my life around. He taught me about faith, hope, and the unconditional love of a Savior.

Bob Castleman lived a very simple life and had minimal needs. He lived in a small cabin on the outskirts of a little town in New Hampshire. To get to the cabin, you had to carefully cross a wooden plank bridge over a brook. As you stepped, peering through the cracks underfoot, you would see the water rushing over stones and massive rocks. You could feel the water splash up onto your feet, which created a sense of being baptized by God Himself.

The lush forest that covered the bridge leading to the north entrance of the cabin created a canopy of green. Maples, mighty oaks, white birches, and pines all intertwined with colors and majesty. It felt as if you were entering into a very sacred place adorned by creation made just for you.

The cabin was concise but livable. One large room consisted of a sitting area, kitchen, and small table. It also had an attached sunroom. The small bathroom that was in one corner had an eco-friendly peat moss toilet and a large claw-foot tub that got filled with buckets of warm water. The walls were adorned with pine boards, which created a warm and peaceful atmosphere that one could feel as soon as they entered. Under the window benches were book-shelves that were filled to capacity, though the only book ever seen lying out was the Bible.

Mr. Castleman had no need for a regular bed because he slept peacefully and soundly wrapped in the weaving of his Mayan hammock. He compared it to the cradling of a mother's womb or being wrapped in the arms of His loving Father.

Across the room was a small cassette player that would quietly fill the air with the sounds of native flute and nature music. "Tsa'ne Dos'e played one of the best versions of 'Amazing Grace' I have ever heard," said Mr. Castleman one day.

The room smelled of herbs, spices, and essential oils, gifts from the earth provided by Father God. In sight were various stones—amethyst, pyrite, rose quartz, citrine, turquoise, and celestine to name a few. They weren't used for "rituals" as some have taught and corrupted; they were just reminders of the beauty and creation of God's handiwork.

One stone in particular looked like a big rock, but when you looked on the inside, you saw beautiful white crystals that had formed. Mr. Castleman used it as a tool to show what we look like on the outside, compared to the beauty that God sees created on the inside.

The cabin was situated high on a hill, which was evidenced in the shortness of breath visitors experienced hiking up to the wooden bridge. To the east, past about an acre of woods, one could see the beating of massive ocean waves which had carved out bluffs uniquely designed by Creator.

To the west, once down a steep bank, one could see a pond that was continuously filled by fresh spring water. The pond was surrounded by cattails dancing ever so slightly in the wind. The water was stocked with bullheads and gold-fish. It always amused me when Mr. Castleman would bring out some fish food and call the fish to eat. Each time they obediently came to the surface and gobbled everything in sight.

The pond was adorned with pink and white lily pads, and one could see the herons quite often enjoying a fish dinner. Around the edges of the pond were three benches in different areas. Next to one bench there was a beautiful purple beebalm bush, and if you sat quiet long enough, a humming-bird would stop by for a drink of sweet nectar.

Another bench was under a willow where the birds would stop by and sing you a song. The third bench was sitting in the open, directly in the sun and moon light where nothing was hidden in the shadows and the warmth of the sun was like a hug from Creator God. Beyond the pond in the far distance was flattened land as far as the eye could see which was filled with wildflowers, bobolinks, swallows swooping and gliding, deer, coyotes, and an occasional fox.

On the south side of the cabin, the woods were dense and the air was filled with the scent of pines. The woods were alive with song and activity from chickadees, veeries, pileated woodpeckers, squirrels, and chipmunks and a nightly hoot from a barred owl. At the largest tree, a white pine, there was a bench where you could sit and rest your head upon the massive trunk. The stories of the ancient tree were endless, always giving glory to God. It was never worshipped, as some have claimed.

The north, south, east, and west directions were meditative areas where one could sit and talk to God. Each area was unique and would help heal past hurts, as I would later learn from Mr. Castleman.

Chapter 2

Meeting Mr. Castleman

THE DAY I MET MR. CASTLEMAN, I KNEW MY LIFE would change. His piercing eyes reflected a light I had never seen, and it drew me in. He had a gentle, kind, peaceful, commanding voice—one that would calm a storm. He walked into my life with a big, oversized down under leather hat and a smile that would melt anyone's heart. He wore jeans, a jean jacket, and work boots and carried a back-pack.

Mr. Castleman was the kind of person who would cause one to think, "This must be what Jesus is like." He exuded such a love and a peaceful presence that would make you want to sit, listen, and talk to him for hours. I was befuddled, yet intrigued. There was something about him that was different, almost seemingly inhuman, yet he was standing right in front of me.

After a short conversation he told me that he was sent by God to come and see me. I backed away. He continued to speak in reassuring tones, saying that he was there to help. Without me saying a word, I knew that he could see deep into my soul. I was exposed, frightened, and at peace all in the same moment.

He shared with me that he had spent years studying medicinal plants and the Word of God. I could tell from his demeanor that he was confident and at peace with who he was, something I immediately envied. Not much more was said after that initial greeting, and he soon said goodbye.

At the time, I owned and operated a small book shop called Journey's in the town of Graceville, a small coastal town in New Hampshire with a population of less than a thousand. It was barely thriving, and with the introduction of the new mega bookstores like Barnes & Nobel and B. Dalton, I knew it was just a matter of time before Journey's would have to close.

Journey's was quaint and before its time. It had sitting areas with big overstuffed chairs for reading, small café-style tables and chairs for sipping coffee or tea. Customers could hear the trickle of water from a fountain I made out of rocks, which added another level of peace to the atmosphere.

A local bakery provided muffins, scones, and a selection of cookies, and the aromas would fill the air, reminding you of home. The warmth, peace, and camaraderie felt when you walked in helped each patron slip away for a time into another world, forgetting the hustle and bustle of time-crunched commitments.

On occasion Journey's hosted mic night for a taste of "coffee house music" and, when lucky, acquired an author to stop by for a signing. The book selections were mostly non-fiction and self-help, with some fiction and a few Bibles scattered here and there. Patrons were able to purchase relaxing music which played throughout the day in the background and also gift cards, knickknacks, and puzzles. I loved my little shop. Just like the patrons, I was able to block out the world once inside.

After Mr. Castleman left, I started cleaning up, getting ready to close shop for the day. It was then I noticed a small white card, what looked like a business card, sitting on one of the shelves. Perplexed, I picked it up. On it were the initials *B.C.* with a phone number. I set it on the back counter not thinking much about it, only saying, "that was all a bit weird."

Journey's was nestled in the middle of the town along Main Street with other mom-and-pop shops. Though the buildings were attached on both sides, they were each unique in color and design. They were akin to the style of the Victorian Painted Ladies only one quarter of the size.

On each side of Journey's, the shops were active with customers. One side was a florist and the other side was an arts and crafts shop. Graceville was self-reliant with its own grocery center, dry cleaners, liquor store, bakery, bar, and my favorite, the Corner Diner.

I was always amazed that there was a church of every denomination in our little town—Roman Catholic, Methodist, Baptist, Full Gospel, Pentecostal—and there was even a Jewish synagogue. The population of Graceville being so small, one would think there were just too many places of worship, but it seemed to fulfill everyone's needs. I made it a point to stay away from all of them because each one felt their way was the right and only way. To me they had God in a box and the likes of me would never be accepted.

Throughout the next few weeks I saw Mr. Castleman walking around through town. Sometimes he was carrying a grocery sack, other times just strolling through with a walking stick. As curiosity piqued, I asked around town if anyone knew who he was. Most shrugged, stating he was quiet, kept to himself, lived to the north of town up on the hill, and walked everywhere he went. The common view was he was an inexplicable stranger, mysterious and eccentric, so people avoided him yet oddly knew enough to gossip about him.

Chapter 3

My Story

I WAS BORN AND RAISED ON A RESERVATION IN
Northern North Dakota in a small community, home to the Ojibway
people. I couldn't wait to leave and get away from the injustices and
poverty of my people. Nothing seemed to change day after day, year after
year. The Ojibway people were poor, undereducated, and depressed—no
fault of their own. They lived in hopelessness, desperation, and third-
world conditions. I watched my parents struggle to provide for us, but
the odds were stacked against them. Drinking became the norm to
numb life's dealings, suicide was an escape for others, and drugs were
rampant. In these conditions, loneliness and despair become too much
to bear.

You cannot blame my brothers and sisters for their choices. They
saw trust broken many times. They were an isolated people. They didn't
belong in the "white man's world" nor in the one the government
created for them. My Native relatives across the land were the only
people who didn't have a choice, a country, or a place to call home.

Hopelessness was an epidemic. I was determined to leave as soon as I could. I worked many long hours finding any odd jobs that would bring in some money. I stashed away money each time I could, but most of it went to help support my family. I didn't finish high school because the building was in disrepair, teachers and supplies were lacking, and in reality, no one really cared and neither did I. Fortunately, I always had a veracious desire to read, which aided me in pursing work and helped me escape into a different world amongst the depression.

As the living conditions worsened, the disturbingly high suicide rates increased rapidly. I watched in horror as another one was reported, this time a twelve-year-old boy who lived on the reservation down the road from me. I went to school with his sister; it was heartbreaking contemplating what she was going through. I saw young people huffing gas, doing drugs, and drinking until they passed out to ease their pain. If I did not leave, I knew I would join the ranks of them.

In my early twenties, I saw an opportunity to get out and took it. One of my cousins was a lucky one; she was fortunate to break out of this vicious cycle by acquiring a scholarship to a college in the United States, a rare feat. I convinced her to let me tag along. My only goal was to get out and never go back. I didn't care where I was going as long as I got out. I prepared, got the necessary paperwork, and gathered all the money I had. I left, never to look back on that life again.

My cousin's school was on the East Coast, in Massachusetts, so I asked her to drop me off at the local bus station. My heart's desire had always been to see the ocean, so after finding an ad for a clerk in a small book shop and checking my remaining funds, I headed to New Hampshire. I think back now and thank God that having a persistent and tenacious personality provided well for me. When I set my mind to do something, it remained set until I accomplished it.

When I arrived in New Hampshire, I was in awe of my new surroundings. Graceville being such a small town, I quickly found the book shop and met the owner, Mrs. Gregory. She was a sweet elderly lady with silver hair and the bluest eyes I had ever seen. She was a widow and never had any children. She welcomed me with open arms, even with my dark complexion and jet black eyes and hair.

She had a small room above the book shop and offered me room and board as long as I helped her run the book shop. It was, for me, a miracle! I settled into my new life learning every aspect of running a small book shop. I remained somewhat secluded and wary of people. As I slowly warmed up, I always made sure my wall of protection was up and intact. I did not talk about my past, and no one inquired seeing that I was different. Fear on both sides I guess.

Life was pretty good for ten years or so. I learned all I could, and Mrs. Gregory became my family. She tried to talk to me about my past, but I was determined to live life with no thoughts about my family, the reservation, or the past life I'd left behind. She respected that; however, I could see the pain in her eyes. She had come to love me as her own, and her heart broke not being able to help me.

Soon that dreaded day was upon me. Mrs. Gregory passed unexpectedly. I was now alone, not knowing what would become of me. Not long after, a lawyer entered the book shop and said he needed to talk to me. Shaken, I sat down figuring he was putting the shop up for sale and I had to get out, but to my surprise, it was the opposite. Mrs. Gregory had named me as her sole survivor and willed the shop and what funds she had saved to me. Stunned, I said nothing. The lawyer kept asking if I was alright, and when I came to my senses I said, "Yes, just shocked."

A year from Mrs. Gregory's passing, I was managing the shop well enough, but the loneliness and heartache from missing her was great. I had no one. Realizing that I could now lose Journey's too because the big corporate book stores were taking over the market was more than I could handle. I went through my days numb. A few patrons tried to reach out to me to no avail. A few good-intentioned Christians approached me but basically pushed me further away with their threats that I was going to hell because I did not know their Jesus.

I thought many times of just running like I had from the reservation, but what would I do? Where would I go? I had a fleeting thought of contacting my family but knew that would only seal the deal on life for me. The shop had closed for the day, and with my head down on my arms in despair, I saw, slightly sticking out from under the register, a card. I pulled it out and saw it was a business card with the letters *B.C.* and a phone number.

I was puzzling over this, then suddenly my head shot up when I realized the *B.C.* stood for Bob Castleman! I thought how strange it was that I had found this after all those years—had to be ten years at least. How bizarre was that!

Chapter 4

My Journey Begins

AS IF THINGS COULDN'T GET WORSE, A FEW DAYS later I had extreme pain in my leg and went to the ER. The doctor said, "It's a blood clot. Good news, it's not a deep vein clot, only a surface blood clot. But if it's not better in three to four days we'll have to operate." I limped back to the shop more discouraged than ever. I had no medical insurance and this would surely destroy me.

Again seeing the *B.C.* card, I remembered Mr. Castleman saying he studied medicinal herbs. I knew from my upbringing that herbs and plants had many healing properties, but that was all I knew. I then did the unthinkable, something entirely unlike myself. Not knowing for sure if he was still in the area and holding my breath, I picked up the phone and I called him.

Mr. Castleman answered and was very kind and gracious. He said he remembered me and suggested I wrap my leg with pieces of wilted cabbage. "Wilt them in the microwave or on top of the stove, but be careful they aren't too hot" he instructed. "Then put the leaves on your leg and wrap your leg with an ace bandage or vet wrap."

He said he would stop in and check on me in a few days. To my surprise, Mr. Castleman actually stopped by! I shared with him that within twenty minutes the pain had subsided and I felt something funny in my leg. I took off the wrap to find the blood clot had burst, and the pain was gone by the next day, just leaving a nasty looking bruise.

From that moment on, Mr. Bob Castleman became my mentor, my teacher, my friend. He would lead me into a new wonderful world, a place of love, healing, and forgiveness. The process was slow, and thankfully he took extra care not to overstep boundaries because he knew that would frighten me off.

For a while he would stop by the shop to say hello and we would just chitchat over casual things. One day when he stopped, he asked me to come for a visit sometime to his cabin. He talked about it with such admiration that it enticed me to step out of my safety zone.

One would think that a woman in her thirties would not go to a cabin alone with an older man, but for some reason there was peace and a comfort of self-assurance. After all our talks I felt as if I knew him, but I also figured it was okay because I had been a fighter back in the day.

On the reservation, or as some would call it, "the Rez," men often took advantage of Native women. I knew how to fight because the government, police, and Rez security officers either didn't care or had their hands full. Most of us girls learned how to protect ourselves because we had to. Sadly, some women would lose the battle and sometimes their lives through the abuse or random abductions . . . an atrocity that still is happening today.

I will never forget that day when I first visited Mr. Castleman. His directions were clear and succinct, and I found myself entering a long, winding path that led me up a steep hill to a wooden bridge. I carefully stepped across the planks as I noticed the rushing brook flowing underneath. Leery of everything, I moved forward stepping slowly so as to avoid tripping or falling. One would think being of Native heritage I would have knowledge of the woods; however, where we lived there was nothing but desolate, dry land that couldn't produce a crop if someone's life depended on it.

Mr. Castleman was waiting at the end of the path, standing before a unique, beautiful little cabin. Instead of taking me inside, he said, "Let's stroll through the woods." He wanted to show me his pond, which would soon become a favorite spot of mine. Mr. Castleman began talking to me about God, Creator of the world, and all that He has done for us. I immediately put up my defenses thinking about the Creator I knew and wondering how He could allow us to be pushed to reservations and live in such inhumane circumstances. Mr. Castleman, noticing I was becoming withdrawn, decided to take another approach.

He then began telling me about Native teachings he learned traveling the world. He explained most Native cultures believed the cardinal directions consisted of different earthly elements. Being so far removed from my customs and traditions, this intrigued me to learn what other cultures taught. I asked him to tell me more, feeling this was a safe subject. We headed further west and came upon this beautiful pond. The water was peaceful and serene; in fact, it reflected what I saw in Mr. Castleman. He was such a peaceful person, slow and steady in his talk, filled with unconditional love. I clearly saw the love he had for God, a God whom I never knew. He would call God "Abba" (which means Father) quite often. He explained that there are many names for God, such as Creator and Lord, but that his favorite was Abba.

We sat on a bench and continued to discuss the four directions that God had created and how powerful and loving God is. I brought the conversation back to my comfort zone and asked what the Native's view was of the west. Mr. Castleman said some believed the west's element was water.

He continued by saying when a person was in turmoil in life, silently sitting by water helped heal the soul. He also added that different types of water helped in different situations. If you were quiet and listened to the small voice inside, he said, God would guide you as to what type of water you needed. It could be a babbling brook, a still, calm pond, a waterfall, or the majesty of the ocean—God would direct you if you asked.

I listened and didn't say a word. The only thing I knew was that sitting at that pond, I felt what must have been peace for the first time in my life. Mr. Castleman continued by telling me that past hurts, fears, shame, regrets all need to be dealt with in order to heal the soul to find inner peace.

He further explained that God created man with a soul. The soul is where your emotions are, your source of feelings, your mind and thoughts. He said that if I had past issues I needed to work through, hitting two sticks together would help release the anger and break the cycle of the past. I was intrigued. That was the first of many meetings to come.

As I left, Mr. Castleman said I could stop by anytime to sit at the pond. Before I left, he blessed me with two beautiful wooden sticks that I could use for some soul work. The sticks were wrapped in leather strips on one end and had beautiful feathers hanging from them along with some beads. I graciously accepted and headed home thinking no way would I use those sticks.

Chapter 5

Healing My Broken Life

A FEW DAYS LATER, I NOTICED THE SALES IN THE book shop continuing to drop, and it was becoming a greater concern. Anxiety and fears were creeping in, and I noticed the wooden sticks lying on the counter. With nothing else to do, I picked up the sticks and started hitting them together. To my surprise, it felt good, and with so much pent up, I hit them harder and harder. Mr. Castleman said it would help break past issues—anger, regrets, and pain—and I had to admit, it really helped! My anxiety subsided, and I even thought for a split second, *I might be able to leave all my problems to Mr. Castleman's God.* Wow, where had that come from? No way would I trust someone I couldn't see!

My lessons continued with Mr. Castleman. He taught me so much. To the east of the cabin we walked through a thicket of woods and ventured upon a cliff overlooking the ocean. From this view, the ocean appeared such a massive body of water. The power of the waves hitting the cliffs made impressions that I likened to art work. I noticed a fire pit with benches around it and learned that some of my Native people would attribute fire to the east, which made sense with the sun rising in the east. I was beginning to see that this God was creative, powerful, and everywhere if I would just open my eyes and heart.

We sat around the fire many evenings talking about God's creation, all of it—mankind, animals, nature, earth, water, wind, and fire. Mr. Castleman shared that some Native cultures believed wearing bells, walking, and singing was a great way to awaken passion and vision in one's life. It was certainly something to ponder. Mr. Castleman had such a way with words that I began to want to hear more about his God. He told me, "Soon, very soon, you will be ready to hear about the greatest love story there ever was."

I found that with all the walks we took, all our talks by the fire and time sitting by the pond, a deep change was taking place in my soul. My emotions were shifting. The peace I had been feeling was increasing, and this was a whole new experience for me.

One of our walks was behind the south side of Mr. Castleman's cabin, which was thick with woods. For some Native cultures, the south represented the earth, and it was a place of healing. As we walked and talked, the earth was fragrant with the smell of pines. I felt the coolness of the woods and the birds singing with joy. Mr. Castleman had a bench near a huge white pine, and he told me the story of how the white pine was significant to the Native American Haudenosaunee; it was the tree of peace. Each bunch of needles had five needles, which represented the uniting of five warring nations—Mohawk, Oneida, Onondaga, Cayuga, and Seneca. Later Tuscarora was added and all are now governed by the Six Nations Council of Iroquois Confederacy.

He then shared stories about medicinal plants that are found throughout the woods and fields. He stated his favorite plant was mullein, a great plant for helping with congestion. He said, "You can dry and steep the leaves to make a tea or smoke them." I was again amazed at what could be found in nature. Maybe hearing about this God, Creator as some called Him, would be safe and, if nothing else, thought-provoking.

Sitting by that great tree, Mr. Castleman gave me a gift wrapped in a piece of cloth. Slowly opening it, I was amazed by the colors and patterns. I had seen something like this on the Rez, but never took time to learn what it was. Mr. Castleman said it was a wapum. It was made of small, cylindrical quahog shell beads strung together. "In your Native culture, it can be worn as a decorative belt, and in the past it was used for sending messages and recording peace treaties, pledges, and marriages. It was even used as an exchange for money."

Attached to the wapum was a small pocket knife, the most beautiful knife I had ever seen. Mr. Castleman taught me how to whittle a stick into different shapes. I could not believe how great it felt just whittling, touching the wood, admiring the different grains and wondering what the final creation would be. Interestingly enough, it was almost indicative of the transformation that was happening within me.

As we continued to sit, Mr. Castleman slowly encouraged me to talk about my past by saying it was time to heal. It was time to let go of the past, forgive and reconnect with my family. I respected his opinion but did not rush into following his advice. Knowing my heart was broken, he suggested that I do "a little drum work." I thought that was an odd thing to say.

At my next visit, Mr. Castleman brought out a deer hide that had been prepared with a non-iodized salt and then soaked in water. He showed me how to scrape the hide, remove the hair, and stretch the hide over a round wooden frame. We then made holes in the edges with a hammer and dole, took some strips of hide that we had cut which looked like laces, and pulled the hide around the frame. On the back of the drum Mr. Castleman had me hold a round metal ring so he could weave the lace in and out through the holes to the ring. He then pulled the hide tight until there was no give left. Then he said, "That's it for today. Time for the hide and lace to dry. Please come back in a few days."

Over the next few days my anticipation grew greatly—so much so I mostly ran up the steep hill to Mr. Castleman's cabin when I returned. I was so excited, and seeing the drum was beyond my expectation. It had the most beautiful deep sound. Mr. Castleman then showed me how to color it with Kool-Aid. I chose red and called it my fire drum.

Mr. Castleman was right; I did much healing heart work with that drum. It awakened deep within me a heartbeat of life, and I was feeling more alive than I had ever felt. As I continued my drum work, I realized that all of a sudden I started to have hope for what was a hopeless future.

Chapter 6

A Deeper Walk

THE SEASONS FLEW BY, JOURNEY'S WAS STILL hanging on by a thread. It helped that I offered some classes on things that I learned. As I headed up the hill to the cabin, I stopped and noticed the air—how wonderful it was! I began dancing with joy and picked up some pebbles to shake with my hands cupped together. The rattle sound was beautiful, and I felt as if I was a powerful warrior ready to face the world and all that it had to offer.

I told Mr. Castleman about this when I arrived at the cabin, and he smiled with his eyes. He said, "You see, you have heard that still, quiet voice of God within you, and He whispered the meaning of the last direction that we have not discussed, the north. All that you mentioned are the attributes Natives relate to the north direction—the air, rattle, dancing, and the strength of a warrior." I was speechless, yet beaming inside.

Mr. Castleman then invited me into his cabin. I had been in it a few times but never stayed long. This time he asked me to come sit in a big wicker chair by his reading shelf. As always, I gazed around this tiny space in awe of the items and peace I felt there. I guess I would compare it to what it would be like to be in heaven.

Mr. Castleman first had to put his sun conure parrot, Hadassah, back in the cage, for he allowed her to wander around the house out of the cage until company came. Hadassah had vibrant golden yellow plumage with orange underparts and face. I asked what the name meant, and Mr. Castleman said it was the Hebrew name for Esther implying compassion.

He continued by saying, "In the Bible, the Book of Esther tells the story of a Jewish woman married to the King of Persia who saved her people from extermination." Mr. Castleman suggested that one day I read it, for it had much to do with the path that I was on. I let that comment slide! I still remember Hadassah to this day. Her personality was like a human's. If you talked to her, she responded as if she knew exactly what was being said.

After mentioning the Book of Esther, Mr. Castleman said it was time to go deeper in our talks, and he blessed me with a beautiful leather Bible, stating, "This book will change your life." He explained, "The Bible is the infallible, incorruptible Word of God; it is truth that never changes."

"It consists of thirty-nine books in the Old Testament, which are about the time before Jesus Christ lived, and twenty-seven books in the New Testament, which are about Jesus' life and beyond. Some call the Bible the Word of God; others call it a love letter to His children.

"Without a doubt it is a guide that needs to be used daily by people in order for them to know how to live life to the fullest. It has practical applications for living today, even though written decades ago."

He continued by saying that the Bible was inspired by the Spirit of God through man. I explained to Mr. Castleman that I had some Bibles in my book shop and that I'd tried reading one once but was unable to understand it.

Mr. Castleman said that was okay and understandable. The Bible contained secret truths and hidden messages only for those willing to know God and His Son. He encouraged me and said together we would learn, one step at a time. He also said as I spent time reading the Word of God, meditating in it and writing it on the tablet of my heart, I would come to understand and see.

Mr. Castleman then gave me a brief overview of what the Bible was all about. I listened intently, and since Mr. Castleman had not led me wrong yet, my gut was to trust him in this too.

My first assignment was to read Psalm 91 with Mr. Castleman. He showed me where the Psalms were in the Bible, and together we read:

> *He who dwells in the secret place of the Most High*
> *Shall abide under the shadow of the Almighty.*
>
> *I will say of the LORD, "He is my refuge and my fortress;*
> *My God, in Him I will trust."*
>
> *Surely He shall deliver you from the snare of the fowler*
> *And from the perilous pestilence.*
> *He shall cover you with His feathers,*
> *And under His wings you shall take refuge;*
> *His truth shall be your shield and buckler.*
> *You shall not be afraid of the terror by night,*
> *Nor of the arrow that flies by day,*
> *Nor of the pestilence that walks in darkness,*
> *Nor of the destruction that lays waste at noonday.*
> *A thousand may fall at your side,*

And ten thousand at your right hand;
But it shall not come near you.
Only with your eyes shall you look,
And see the reward of the wicked.

Because you have made the LORD, who is my refuge,
Even the Most High, your dwelling place,
No evil shall befall you,
Nor shall any plague come near your dwelling;
For He shall give His angels charge over you,
To keep you in all your ways.
In their hands they shall bear you up,
Lest you dash your foot against a stone.
You shall tread upon the lion and the cobra,
The young lion and the serpent you shall trample underfoot.

Because he has set his love upon Me, therefore I will
deliver him;
I will set him on high, because he has known My name.
He shall call upon Me, and I will answer him;
I will be with him in trouble;
I will deliver him and honor him.
With long life I will satisfy him,
And show him My salvation.

My mind was whirling. I had never heard words with such depth, filled with so many hidden meanings. I was overwhelmed with all kinds of emotions. I felt fear seeping up deep within me. As usual, my initial reaction was to run, but something kept me there.

I shared with Mr. Castleman that as we began to read the Psalm together, I immediately got stuck on the word *trust*. *Trust,* I thought to myself. That was something greatly lacking in my life. Because of our history, we Natives only knew how to distrust; we were suspicious, cynical, angry, and rightly so. Mistrust was imbedded deeply in my people and well learned by me. Throughout my life I had only trusted two people, and they were Mrs. Gregory, whom I still dearly missed, and now Mr. Castleman.

It would be quite a journey to move from this state of living to love and trust. I questioned silently, *How can I trust this God I cannot see?* This truly perplexed me.

Chapter 7

The Ultimate Gift of Love

AT OUR NEXT MEETING, MR. CASTLEMAN BEGAN by saying, "The ultimate gift in the world that mankind has missed and completely misunderstood is that God loves you! He is not selective, judgmental, or a respecter of persons. It is not based on who you are, the color of your skin, your culture, where you are in life, what you have done or not done. The Bible tells us that God is love. 1 John 4:8 says 'He who does not love does not know God, for God is love.'

"Many will argue that they cannot love the way God loves, but if you really understand that you are created in His image, then you can love as God does." Mr. Castleman continued, "This is where we will begin our next lesson. Your Native people from years past knew of Great Spirit, or Creator God, as some may have called Him. Many heard and were led by Great Spirit and even knew of a 'Savior' that would come. Some interpreted this as a God different from the God in the Bible;

others felt it was the same. That is not the point or where we will focus. It is time you learn how much God loves you by learning about His Son, Jesus.

"In the beginning of time, God created Adam and Eve. They were enticed and deceived to believe they could be like God and chose to not trust Him who created them. Adam and Eve committed a great sin against God, and all mankind loss their ability to commune with God. Because of this, there needed to be a man without sin to be the propitiation, a substitute to atone for man's evil choice, so God sent His Son, Jesus Christ, to save us."

Mr. Castleman continued and said, "Love never fails. It was the amazing grace and love of God that restored our broken relationship through His Son. Jesus became man, born of the Virgin Mary, and walked on this earth for thirty-three and a half years. The last three years of His life were filled with miracles, healings, followers, and persecutions. God or Jesus himself could have stopped that which was to happen or called legions of angels to thwart the inevitable, but God's greater purpose needed to be accomplished for you and me. This was done through the humble devotion and love of Jesus. He was crucified and was buried. Then on the third day He rose from the dead, and He is now seated at the right hand of God, interceding on our behalf daily.

"More than two thousand years later, those who believe in Jesus Christ as the Son of God have a restored relationship with God the Father. Only those who come to know Jesus can know the Father God, the Creator of all things. This is called being born again or saved. It is not something well embraced even today. Many people believe numerous paths lead to God. Sadly, they are wrong. Mr. Castleman shared that one day he heard clearly in a small, quiet voice God say to him, "Know you this, there is only one way and it is through My Son."

Mr. Castleman explained how many different beliefs and religions taught people to be good or do this or that to obtain eternal salvation but that man would always continue to fail. "That which man does through the flesh will reap only what the flesh can achieve," he said. "Jesus is the only path to eternal salvation. It is a relationship with the Father, the Son, and the Holy Spirit.

"Do not confuse this relationship with church rules, dogmas, and the ritualistic ways of the many Christian denominations. A true believer walks the way of Jesus. His first command found in Luke 10:27 states, 'You shall love the Lord your God with all your heart, with all your soul, with all your strength, and with all your mind and your neighbor as yourself.' This is Jesus' greatest command that surpasses all others."

I listened intently, and tears flowed down my face as I tried to comprehend in my mind what was being said, but I couldn't. I knew deep inside I had just heard truth, and it was resonating in my spirit. It was a day I will never forget.

Later that evening in the stillness of my room, I wept uncontrollably. Not really knowing why I was so distraught, I cried out to God, asking Him to forgive me for all my past missteps, for my sins. It was then I took a step of faith and proclaimed Jesus Christ as my Savior.

On my knees, with my head down on my arms, all of a sudden I felt this overwhelming presence of love around me. It was as if I was being embraced by love and cradled in the arms of Father God. Mr. Castleman had told me this sometimes happened but not always. Everyone's experience was different, and there was no "right way." It was an individual experience. He also told me that being saved was not a feeling, it is not based on emotions. It was a faith walk, a faith statement.

I remained in His presence as I drifted to sleep, exhausted from tears and past burdens, to awaken to a new life—one now filled with love, hope, wonderment, and, to my surprise, more lessons.

Chapter 8

The Day

LIFE WITH MR. CASTLEMAN WAS CHALLENGING
yet adventurous, tearful, fulfilling, healing, and joyful. He celebrated
with me concerning my "new birth," and lessons continued digging
deeper and deeper into the Word of God. I could not imagine life
without him, yet I knew that one day it would come. It certainly didn't
come as I expected. No matter, it was still debilitating. As I think back,
I see that I was forewarned by the Holy Spirit, and even Mr. Castleman
himself said, "There has been a paradigm shift." I had no clue what that
meant at the time and chose to ignore it.

As I normally did, I hiked up to the cabin eager and ready for
another lesson or fun adventure. When I crossed the bridge I called out,
but this day there wasn't an answer. I slowly stepped up onto the porch
where many teachings had taken place and peered into the window. My
breath left me for a moment, and my stomach turned. Immediately I
felt fear creep in and panic rise up through my being.

The first thing I saw was that Hadassah was not in her cage and the
walking stick that Mr. Castleman used was gone. I said to myself, *Calm*

down. He must be out for a walk. But in my spirit I knew that was not the case. I slowly stepped inside, and sitting on the table was a note from Mr. Castleman. With my hands shaking, I picked it up, and it read:

> *It is time to move on. My work is done here. You now have*
> *all you will ever need, the ultimate gift of love. Now go*
> *forth; walk the Jesus way, for you are called.*
> *Fondly,*
> *Mr. Bob Castleman A.D.*

That's it? That's all I get after spending all this time with him? He just leaves? He just disappears? Swirling and reeling, I had to sit before I passed out. I was in shock. *How could he?* is all that kept going through my mind. *How could he just leave and not even say goodbye?*

Over and over I read the note, hoping for a clue, anything, but there was nothing. He was gone.

The days swirled by. I was numb. I found myself slowly slipping back into the space I had been in before I met Mr. Castleman. I didn't pick up the Bible. I didn't pray. I was angry at God, Mr. Castleman, and anyone else who crossed my path.

Journey's was struggling, and I did not care. I wallowed and whined even though I now know that was what the Israelites did while in the desert and it got them nowhere. I felt hopeless again. My focus was on me and my situation. I had no peace, joy, or vision for the future . . . again! I had no friends, many fears, and nothing to live for, so I thought.

The Holy Spirit was constantly urging me to go for a walk, but I fought that too. Early one morning, unable to sleep, I again picked up the note left by Mr. Castleman. This time when I read it, my eyes went right to *A.D.* as if it was highlighted by the early morning light. Why hadn't I seen that before?

My mind brought me back to the day I found the business card Mr. Castleman left that said *B.C.* I quickly pulled out my computer, looked up *A.D.*, and learned it stands for *anno Domini*, Latin for "year of our Lord," indicating the number of years since the birth of Jesus Christ. It was the first time in weeks that I'd felt some peace, and a slight smile crossed my face.

The Holy Spirit reminded me that Mr. Castleman was a gift from God; he came to me *B.C.*, before I knew Christ. I was to be grateful for the time we spent together and embrace all the lessons. This was to be my "year of the Lord," which meant it was time to walk the talk and be all God created me to be for His glory and purpose. I wept and asked for forgiveness. I had forsaken God, but He never left me, as promised.

I went for a walk that day to all the familiar places and some new ones being led step by step by the Holy Spirit. He showed me it was time for me to focus on Psalm 46:10: "Be still, and know that I AM God." That is what I did, for days, weeks, and months, until the peace of God fell upon me. It was then I realized that I cannot depend on Mr. Castleman or others to fulfill me or make me happy. It is only through a deep relationship with Jesus Christ that the voids in life can be filled. It truly is the ultimate gift to mankind. The love of God is what would make my life complete.

One quiet summer afternoon, floating on the river in my kayak, I heard very clearly from God what I was to do next with my life. Through the love of Mr. Castleman and the ultimate love of Creator God, I found me. It was time to walk the Jesus way in life and fulfill my purpose. It was time for me to return to my people and share with them the love I had found.

Holy Spirit reminded me of the story of Esther and that Mr. Castleman had said it had much to do with the path I was on. Truly it was time to meditate deeper in the Book of Esther. I now knew that

Abba God, His Word, Holy Spirit, and the love of Yahshua would surely show me the way. Faith steps were all that I needed.

I praised God with drums, rattles, sticks, and song. I lifted my hands with thanksgiving. I danced as David did with my bells and worshiped the King of kings. I had found my purpose, my calling.

I shall always keep Mr. Castleman in my prayers, sending love and strength his way knowing he is fulfilling his next calling in service to the Abba. I have moved beyond anger to thankfulness, complete gratitude, and love for him. I shall never forget him, all he taught and sacrificed for me. I do, however, look forward to the day when we meet again, either in the earthly realm or heavenly realm.

I'm now at peace. Holy Spirit has called me back home to the reservation and has instructed me to teach all I have learned to my people. It is critical. I must share the good news of Creator God, Yahuwah, and His Son, Yahshua, Jesus the Christ. My people must know that they are loved.

My name is Shawana, daughter of Creator God, disciple of Yahshua and blessed to be a "keeper of my people," "Ganawenjige Anishinaabekaa," for the glory of God and His Kingdom.

Chapter 9

Epilogue –
Open Your Hearts

EVERYONE HAS A STORY. LIFE IS A SERIES OF journeys bookended by a past of joy or pain and a future of hope or despair. My prayer is that you gleaned from Shawana's story tidbits of hope and encouragement.

I pray that you have received the life-changing ultimate gift, the love of God and His Son, into your life. You are created in His image and are truly loved.

This journey called life is not an easy one, but it is more bearable with the Creator of all things loving you. Jesus the Christ (Yahshua, Yeshua, or Yahusha as some call Him) sits at the right hand of God and is continuously interceding on our behalf. All you need to do is ask and receive. What a blessing this is! What a gift of love!

In closing, often Abba gives me a word of encouragement, and here is one for you:

Awaken my child, awaken. Open your hearts to the love of My Son and you will come to know Me as well. It is only through Him that we can commune. You only need to believe on Him and you too will become my son or my daughter eternally. I will be your Father forevermore.

Seek not other paths, for the truth lies here in this parable of love. Seek not other people, but dwell in My Word and understanding will be yours.

I have prepared a purpose for each of My children and only by drawing close will you find the way. Only through My Son will you see the way, the truth, and the life that I have ordained for you.

You are my special creation and I love you.

Be still and know Me.

Be of good cheer, for My Son has now set you free.

A Parable of Forgiveness

Dear children,

This parable of forgiveness takes you on a journey through the eyes of First Nations people. It not only applies to these beautiful people, but also to all people in the world who have suffered at the hand of another.

Unresolved forgiveness creates a life of anger, strife, and hatred. Where there is unforgiveness, there can be no peace personally, corporately, or throughout the world.

This parable is for those who are bitter, angry, hurt, lost, and living with no hope. It is for any and all people who have had injustices done to them for the mere fact they exist and were "in the way."

May this parable lift your spirits and bring a new hope to you. May you be renewed with a desire to live life to the fullest and accomplish that which Creator God ordained for you. You are His unique creation, and you are loved.

God's blessings and peace ~

Chapter 1

Walking The Jesus Way

IT TOOK MUCH LONGER THAN I EXPECTED TO wrap up things at my small book shop, Journey's, though I have to admit, I wasn't in any hurry to return back to the reservation even knowing I had a calling on my life to do so.

Kayaking had become a favorite activity for me, and I was concerned that on the reservation I wouldn't have the chance to paddle. I was also deeply concerned I would be drawn back into the world that I had left, losing all I had learned over the past years. I knew deep in my spirit that with this type of thinking I wasn't really trusting Abba and this was just procrastination.

It is amazing how one can easily explain stalling. For me, I kept saying I needed to do this for my health. The closeness of the water always drew me in and brought peace to my body, soul, and spirit.

Whether it was walking, kayaking, or watching God's creation, I found it was something I needed to do daily to remain grounded in Him.

God's creation was a wonder to me, like the herons standing at the water's edge watching for fish or perching high in the trees. It would bring a smile to my face when they gawked at me as I paddled by. The beavers fascinated me with their diligence and unwavering focus on building their dams and gathering food and with how they would slap their flat tails when I got too close. Early morning or late evening was always the best time to watch the beavers, and if fortunate, I was able to watch the baby beavers swim and play.

Once I was blessed to see a family of common merganser ducks. They flew in and landed on the river in a perfectly straight line, ten of them. I chuckled each time their butts stuck up out of the water as they dove before coming up with small white fish in their beaks. They weren't the most colorful ducks I had seen, certainly not like the mallards. The common mergansers had gray-colored heads and crowns, orange beaks, brown bodies, and all white undersides. Regardless, I spent hours watching them.

The lessons I gleaned from those ducks and all of God's creation would sustain me in the most difficult days that were to come.

Sitting in the midst of God's creation always brought to remembrance my dear friend Mr. Castleman. He had a special connection with nature and animals, one beyond most humans. He told me of an owl that was injured as a fledging and how he'd nurtured it back to health. The bond created between the two lasted a lifetime. I will never forget the day I heard the owl calling out. It was early evening, and we were on one of our many hikes. All of a sudden Mr. Castleman called back, and this huge owl came soring down and landed on his extended arm. It was massive yet beautiful. Within minutes it flew away. I was amazed, and Mr. Castleman explained it was like the bond we have with God; it would always be there.

That bond he talked about was similar to the one that I had with him. It was a godly connection. It amused me how often he retold the story of how he was sent to my shop by the leading of the Lord. He had been sitting in his cabin enjoying quiet time reading the Bible, when he clearly heard the Lord say, "Go meet the owner of the small bookshop in town." The day he stepped into my life was the day my life changed.

I had been at a point of desperation and hopelessness. I had no one. I had alienated myself from my family, I had no friends, and the future was bleak. I had inherited a small book shop in the town of Graceville, New Hampshire. For years life was good. Mrs. Gregory, the owner, had become my family when she took me in without question. I had traveled far from home, desperate to get out and insistent on never going back. I grew up on a small rural reservation in Northern North Dakota, home to the Ojibway people. I never felt I belonged there, and now I didn't belong in Graceville either.

Mr. Castleman thought otherwise, though. He became my mentor, a teacher of life. The minute he stepped into the shop and I saw in his eyes his unconditional love and light, I thought, *That is something I want and need.* Mr. Castleman diligently taught me over a span of almost three years before he was called to another assignment. Daily he would call or stop in to see me. It was as if he knew exactly where I was emotionally, spiritually, and physically. It was something that frightened me at first; however, I learned it was really God my Father watching over me through His faithful servant.

Mr. Castleman gently and lovingly taught me some of my native heritage and showed me that God loves all His people, no matter color, race, or creed. This was made evident by His Son and the work of the cross. It was Mr. Castleman who talked to me without judgment,

45

unlike others who supposedly were sharing the "good news." It was his Christlike love, the kind of love that accepted me for who I was, that led me to want to know who Jesus Christ was. I will always remember the day when Jesus, or Yahshua, which I like to call Him, became my Savoir, my life, my all in all.

After that life-changing moment and all the teachings Mr. Castleman gave me, there was a paradigm shift. I didn't recognize it immediately, but I came to find myself strong and able to stand on my own. The change? I had Jesus. I found the love of my Father, and I had the Word of God to live by. Knowing all this did not stop me from being devastated the day Mr. Castleman disappeared, but though I reeled from that shock for months, I knew deep in my heart that I now had a calling and purpose.

Before Mr. Castleman left, he told me I was to spend time in the Book of Esther. Knowing he did not say anything without a reason or cause, I did exactly as he suggested. The lessons I gleaned from Esther ignited deep within me the desire to save my people; they taught me how to step out in faith even through fears, as Esther did. God provided her a means to save her people, and I too had that calling as "keeper of my people." It was now time to head back home to the reservation and share what it meant to walk through life the Jesus way.

Chapter 2

Remembering My Past

MR. CASTLEMAN TAUGHT ME THAT WITHOUT recognition there cannot be forgiveness, without forgiveness there is no reconciliation, and without reconciliation there is no peace. This was the life that I had been born into on the reservation some thirty years prior—a life of no peace, a life of no hope.

There was no one to blame, yet there was everyone to blame. Through my healing journey I learned it was essential that I stop hiding my head in the sand by intentionally ignoring the past. It was time to embrace my culture; it was time to research my Native history and learn the truth instead of blindly believing what had been taught to me by the ill-equipped schools—if they could even be called that with their lack of books and teachers on—the Rez. The elders knew the truth. They tried to teach the younger generations, but the bitterness and anger was beaten down by drinking and drugs to numb the pain and forget the past, and the future too for that matter.

It was at this crucial time in my life that I recognized the true history and sufferings of my people. This was the moment I began my journey to forgiveness. I finally understood it wasn't the fault of my parents, whom I had continuously blamed. It hadn't started with them or what I saw happening daily on the Rez. I realized they were all suffering too.

It had started generations back. The defeated attitude and lack of belonging began when my Native race was considered less than any other man, when we were considered inferior or, as some would say, "savages." It began back in history when Columbus discovered our country and we were captured, made slaves, and killed. It was all about money—gold, spices, and the riches that were found in our land. When we were in the way, we were removed.

Indigenous people, Native Americans, First Nations people as we are called today, had a great respect for God's creation. We shared properties, lived in villages, and did everything together. Women took care of the crops and the children; men would hunt for food. We were taught to respect our elders, and honor was given to Creator. This was in great contrast to the European values of greed, self-gratification, and self-preservation. Columbus did not enter a land of savages and wilderness; he entered a land of people who honored Creator God, who cared for each other and worked together as people should.

As Columbus traveled around the Caribbean capturing First Nations people, the Arawaks, word spread throughout the villages. Soon my people began to fight back, as women and children were being taken as slaves for sex and labor. If gold could not be found, then my people were punished, hunted down and killed.

Columbus reassured himself that what he was doing was righteous and God-driven. He was full of religious talk to explain away the truth of complete annihilation. After Columbus and the Spaniards' arrival, the population of Native Arawaks went from 250,000 to around 500 in just fifty years.

I was distraught and wept at the statistics I was finding. As I continued, I told myself this research must be done so mankind could recognize the injustices, so we as a people could move forward to overcome the abuse and move to forgiveness. It was gut-wrenching, but necessary.

Throughout history, European Americans have continued to condemn other cultural groups for not changing their heritage and customs to integrate into "the American lifestyle"; however, the rationalizations given for what was done to the First Nations people, a peaceful people, were atrocious. Bounties were put on my people's heads, which varying from $25 to $130 for a male scalp, and it was usually half that amount for a woman's or child's. It was said the only good Indian was a dead one. As I read this I realized that this attitude has been common for over 400 years.

As I dug deeper into history, the abuse and destruction of my Native people and their culture perpetuated. To recount all the injustices would be impossible; however, I feel it is necessary to cover a couple of them for the healing process.

First, the Trail of Tears. The Cherokee Nation was given two years to leave the land they occupied, but many wanted to stay in their homeland. Seven thousand troops were sent to remove the people in 1830. They were made to march hundreds of miles to what is now Oklahoma. They were forced at bayonet-point and held in stockades. About 4,000 died from hunger, disease, and the trek through treacherous, cold territory. This atrocity was sanctioned by the US government because someone wanted the land.

Recently, I saw an article about students hanging a banner for a sports function that read, *Hey Indians, how about a trail of tears, round 2?* The school officials handled this well; however, I clearly saw the ignorance of people and the need to recognize the importance of resolutions across the nation. Clearly, the healing has not begun, people are insensitive and unaware of the truth. Compassion is desperately lacking.

And then there is the massacre at Wounded Knee. Around 1888, the remaining Sioux were forced to reservations at gun point. Though they were broken physically and spiritually, an awakening began in the North American tribes. A holy man had received a message from Creator that they would soon be free from the white man. Hope grew, excitement broke out, and some became defiant of the holy man's belief of nonviolence. A ritual called the Ghost Dance spread through the north, and fearing a rebellion, the settlers of South Dakota commanded the ritual dance be discontinued. When this was ignored, the US Army interceded.

As tempers and fears escalated, about 300 Sioux left the reservation and hesitantly agreed to be moved to Wounded Knee Creek, the Pine Ridge Reservation. On December 29, 1890, a gun was mistakenly fired when the army commanded surrendering Sioux weapons, and the Seventh Cavalry aggressively fired on the Sioux. Chief Big Foot was shot in his tent; others were killed as they tried to run away. Almost all of the 300 men, women, and children were shot dead. Others died frozen in the snow.

This was about 400 years after Columbus came to this "uninhabited" land. The massacre at Wounded Knee was the last confrontation between First Nations people and the United States Army. In 1890, the United States census affirmed the frontier was now officially closed.

Throughout the years, the government felt their proposal to permanently remove my people to government-run reservations was for their protection. The goal was to civilize my people until they were assimilated into the white man's culture.

We were encouraged to integrate and adapt to American culture.

The intent was to improve tribal life. However, this did more destruction than good, and it continues today throughout the nation. Alaskan villages have the highest suicide rate per capita in the United States, a suicide rate of almost four times the national average. The more youth are exposed to suicidal behavior, the more likely many more will become "just a statistic" to the rest of the world.

Extremely high suicide rates exist on my reservation and many other tribal reservations such as South Dakota, Montana, and Arizona to name a few. Suicides are not only rampant amongst young children and teens, even parents, aunts, and uncles succumb and choose suicide to escape the deplorable conditions.

Many First Nations people live in extreme poverty with little or no electricity and contaminated or no running water. A documentary was recently released exposing the harsh living conditions of the Blackfeet whose land was made a wasteland from drilling oil. It was discovered the government was cheating the land holders of millions of dollars, and a lawsuit was filed by Elouise Cobbell against the United States for proper retribution.[1] These inhumane conditions and injustices need to be recognized and addressed before healing and forgiveness and can be achieved. The first step is admitting to the problems.

Annihilation of the First Nations people may have been the original objective, and technically it happened because our bodies, souls, and spirits were destroyed. After that, what is left? History proves we became a people without self-value, without a home, without a country, and it still continues today.

---

[1] Documentary "100 Years; One Woman's Fight for Justice": https://www.netflix.com/title/80144983

51

Chapter 3

Journey To My People

THE DAY FINALLY CAME WHEN I CLOSED UP Journey's and my belongings were packed. Before leaving Graceville, I took once last walk up to Mr. Catstleman's cabin, hoping he had come back and I would find him there. I was only disappointed and sad when I saw no signs of life. But the cabin was still in good shape considering it had been empty for a season or two, and the peace I had always felt there was still present.

I walked to a few of my favorite spots for one last look. As usual, I was blessed by the walk through God's creation. The benches at the pond were welcoming, and I sat for a while on the bench that was situated in the sun. I soaked up the warmth because I was chilled after walking through the cool, shady woods. The heat from the sun warmed not only my physical body but also my spiritual being. As I bathed in this moment, the presence of the Lord came upon me, and I heard the Lord clearly saying to me:

My daughter the time is now. You have a great work to be done, and I am calling you. For far too long unforgiveness has blocked blessings on My people. One cannot walk in love and hold bitterness in his or her heart. The greatest command given to mankind is to love one another as I have loved you. This cannot happen if there is strife and unforgiveness throughout the land.

You have learned much. You are ready, and I will be with you each step of the way. The journey may not be easy, but it is critical.

A great awakening has started, and in order for that to continue there must be forgiveness. My Son at the cross prepared the way, but mankind has gotten distracted from His finished work, from My love, from My way. Go forth My daughter. Fulfill that which I ordained from the beginning of time. Be still and listen for guidance. Go forth in peace.

My heart pounded in my chest. I knew it was the voice of God and I must be about my Father's business. I headed back to the shop, picked up my bag, and made the next bus connection to North Dakota. The route was over twenty-eight hours with at least four stops, so I settled in for my journey home. I took this time to mediate in the Word, listen for instructions from the Holy Spirit, and rest and pray and bathe in His presence. It had been many years since I was back home, and not being sure of what kind of reception I would get, I was a bit apprehensive. Casting my care on Him, though, I was reassured with Isaiah 61:1–3:

The Spirit of the Lord GOD is upon Me,
Because the LORD has anointed Me
To preach good tidings to the poor;
He has sent Me to heal the brokenhearted,
To proclaim liberty to the captives,
And the opening of the prison to those who are bound;
To proclaim the acceptable year of the LORD,
And the day of vengeance of our God;
To comfort all who mourn,
To console those who mourn in Zion,
To give them beauty for ashes,
The oil of joy for mourning,
The garment of praise for the spirit of heaviness;
That they may be called trees of righteousness,
The planting of the LORD, that He may be glorified.

The trip went faster than I'd expected, and soon I would be stepping back in time, to a time I would just as soon forget if it weren't for my calling from Creator God. To prepare, I recalled what I had researched in current articles in print and on the internet prior to leaving.

My home was one of the largest First Nations communities. The reservation had a population of between 2,300 and 3,000 living on just under 4,500 acres. The Ojibway people valued their way of life, their language, family, and traditions.

What had once been a thriving community that flourished by hunting, trapping, fishing, gathering, and living on the land, was now a community in crisis. Statistics reported that an estimated 75% of the population was under twenty-five and unemployment was over 90%. The entire population lived in about 375 homes. Due to the lack of housing, families needed to sleep in shifts. A diesel generator provided power to the community, and 80% of the homes did not have clean running water or sewage systems.

I'd heard that the reservation's only school had burned to the ground in 2007 but was encouraged when I read a new one had been built in 2016. Life was hard on the Rez. There was no work, inadequate education, and no healthcare or security, and there had been a boil water advisory for over ten years due to the lack of power from the generator. Alcoholism, domestic abuse, depression, drug use, solvent abuse, and sniffing gas had become a way of life for many. Often, women were abused or simply disappeared. I had run when the suicide rate hit an all-time high because I knew I could be next.

I had read that the community would soon have a mental worker for every 100 residents, which was great, but the root cause still needed to be addressed. I also learned that 27 million dollars was being provided by the federal government to connect our reservation to the power grid. I wondered how long that would take to happen. Not trusting what we were told was an inherited trait among us Natives, something we all learned from generations before us.

I lived in a remote rural community accessible only by airplane and a few un-kept roads. All the counseling in the world couldn't help with the fact that my people needed to be able to work and provide for their families. Our community grew fast when federal subsidies were provided, but with the subsidies came the deterioration of living conditions and violent crime.

Federal government believed what they were doing was helpful for all tribes across the United States. They said their intent was to help; however, I believe this was the root cause of my people's demise—what happened to my relatives not too far back in history.

Our land was taken from us, and we were moved to reservations.

Christian missionaries came in and urged or forced my people to abandon old traditions. Elders who had lived through it talked openly about the boarding schools run by Christian missionaries. They described how the missionaries took Native children from their families and put them in the schools. They cut the children's hair, changed their clothes, and beat them if they spoke their Native language. The missionaries did everything they could to assimilate us into the "white man's world." We were crushed; our spirits were broken and our souls were destroyed. We belonged nowhere, had no dignity, and our self-worth was annihilated.

I remembered reading a statement by Clyde Warrior, a Ponca and the President of the National Indian Youth Council in 1967. He captured the life of my people with his words:

> *Most [of us] . . . can remember when we were children and spent many hours at the feet of our grandfathers listening to stories of the time when the Indians were a great people, when we were free, when we were rich, when we lived the good life.*
>
> *At the same time we heard stories of droughts, famines and pestilence. It was only recently that we realized that there was surely great material deprivation in those days, but that our old people felt rich because they were free.*
>
> *They were rich in the things of the spirit, but if there is one that characterizes Indian life today it is poverty of the spirit. We still have human passions and depth of feeling, but we are poor in spirit because we are not free - free in the most basic sense of the word.*

*We are not allowed to make those basic human choices
and decisions about our personal life and about the destiny
of our communities which is the mark of free mature
people. We sit on our front porches or in our yards, and
the world and our lives in it pass us by without our desires
or aspirations having any effect.*

*We are not free. We do not make choices. Our choices are
made for us; we are the poor . . . We have many rulers . . .
They call us into meetings and tell us what is good for us
and how they've programmed us, or they come into our
homes to instruct us and their manners are not always
what one would call polite by Indian standards or perhaps
any standards.*

*We are rarely accorded respect as fellow human beings. Our
children come home from school to us with shame in their
hearts and a sneer on their lips for their home and parents.*

*We are the "poverty problem" and that is true; and perhaps
it is also true that our lack of reasonable choices, our lack
of freedom, our poverty spirit is not unconnected with our
material poverty.*[2]

---

[2] Wilson, 370-371, Wilson, James. The Earth Shall Weep. New York, NY: Gove Press, 1999.

Chapter 4

Reconnecting

SURELY I NEVER WOULD HAVE EXPECTED TO BE hugged so tightly that I could hardly breathe and that the tears would fall freely from my family member's eyes. I wept as I hugged each one of them, so happy to see them yet ashamed and full of remorse for the way I'd left.

It was a moment I will always remember, for I was embraced as the prodigal son was in Luke 15:20: "And he arose and came to his father. But when he was still a great way off, his father saw him and had compassion, and ran and fell on his neck and kissed him." Abba is good and faithful!

We spent quite a bit of time catching up and sharing a meal of my favorites—"fry bread" and "three sister's soup" (corn, beans, and squash). I was amazed how comfortable I felt and reveled in the fact that all the anger and anxiety I'd had when I left was now gone. I quietly thanked Yahshua for His peace that surpassed all my understanding.

I was ever so grateful too that there was a room for me to share with one of my sisters. She had been a young girl when I left, so I was hoping we could catch up and get to know each other. This was not an easy process, but Creator managed to break down the walls that were between us.

I did not yet bring up my salvation and that I now walked the Jesus way. From my experience I knew it was crucial not to push. Abba showed me to just let my love and light shine and as time went on He and the Holy Spirit would create the perfect opportunities to share.

My dad was still mostly unemployed, and I could see the pain in his eyes. The inability to provide for one's family shatters self-esteem; it surely has brought many men into deep depressions in all walks of life. I was thankful that my dad had not given up and daily looked for work. Occasionally he found it. My mom was still the keeper of the home and did an amazing job considering the lack of essentials, clean water and heat, and the fact that daily she had to deal with a roof over-head that leaked. I realized that my family had a determination that some of my Ojibway brothers and sisters lacked. I was grateful for that. It was something I had not seen before I left.

One afternoon I was able to talk to my youngest sister, Aki, and hear from her perspective what life had been like on the Rez. With tears in her eyes, she shared how a school friend, fifteen years old, had just committed suicide. Aki continued by saying that he left behind parents who recently had lost another son and nephew and that there were also four more teens who had committed suicide earlier that month. Normally her classmates would handle this by huffing gas, getting drunk, or recklessly driving at high speeds to get away and shut down the pain, but this time they made a different choice.

A group of about thirty teens decided instead of diving into the darkness of grief and despair to get together and help the families that had lost children. They cooked meals, ran errands, cleaned, cut grass, fixed broken items, and gathered clean water in jugs for the families. Aki said it was such an amazing sight. The focus was to be selfless instead of selfish, and it lifted their spirits more than huffing gas.

I was pleased to see this positive movement in some of the youth, but without Yahshua they had a long way to go. The Holy Spirit reminded me, though, it was not time yet and directed me to go visit with the elders.

This time I saw my elders with different eyes, with the eyes of Jesus. Judgments had fallen by the wayside, and a spirit of love and compassion filled my being. My heart broke as I listened to them sharing stories of their past. After the government and Christian missionaries invaded our land to "rescue" my people, the atrocities and alienations continued. And they were still continuing to that day.

I listened as my uncle told the story of how he had learned long ago from his elders of a Savior that would come and walk amongst the people. "When the missionaries came," he said, "many were excited, hoping this might be the Savior we heard about long ago. However, as the different missionaries came and shared about Jesus, along with them came many different interpretations of the Bible and denominations. Our people became confused as the different missionaries told them 'No the Baptists are wrong. The only path to Savior is the Methodist denomination.' It was the same for Roman Catholics and any others who came to rescue us."

I couldn't even imagine how that must have been. They weren't taught about the love of Savior, of a loving Father as I was. My uncle continued, telling me how one day he decided to check out a little white Lutheran church not too far from where he lived. As he entered, he was greeted with looks and whispers, for his clothes and hair were different from the rest. He sat in the back, knowing that would be the only place he could sit inconspicuously, but even that didn't work.

He felt ashamed and unloved. After the service, the pastor talked to him about "fitting in better" by dressing appropriately. From that day on, my uncle never set foot in a church. He went home and tried to rub the color of his skin off, so desiring to fit in and be loved. He was searching for and wanting to learn about a Savior, but he only found rejection.

One may think that this happened generations ago, but that is not the case. I felt the same when I was in Graceville. Most would look at me strangely and had the stereotypical preconception that I was a "lazy, no good Indian." I was blessed by the people God brought into my life who were not of that manner.

It saddened me deeply that my people were still not accepted and felt so hopeless, ashamed, and abused. I understood their anger, but I had overcome it and knew there was hope! I knew a Savior that came to save the lost and unloved, and soon I would share this openly with my people.

Chapter 5

Building Bridges of Trust

I UNDERSTAND HOPELESSNESS, ABUSE, ANGER, and despair. I grew up with it. I understand the lack of trust buried within a soul. These shackles run deep through generations of people. The bonds appear in life as guilt, shame, skepticism, rejection, loneliness, insecurity, and the feeling of worthlessness. A life filled with these burdens is a life without hope that leads to depression, addictions, heartbreaks, and sadly, death.

My people's past was imbedded in their souls, for they lived with these bondages daily, and it broke my heart. However, as I had come to find, Jesus could and would free them from this past. Mr. Castleman taught me that reconciliation was an instrumental part of healing and restoration, not just for my people but for any cultural group or person that was treated inhumanely.

I learned that walking the Jesus way and with the Word, one could learn to take past injustices and deep, soulful wounds and move toward building bridges of forgiveness. One evening in my prayer time, the Holy Spirit started to give me instructions as to how this healing process was to begin. He instructed that the walls must be broken down with love and compassion and that I must take this journey with them.

Self-work is not easy. Looking into our own souls exposes things that we are not proud of at times, and it is easier to just walk away. The shame and insecurity wall must be cracked, though, so one can realize that Jesus loves them unconditionally just the way they are. Thankfully, the Holy Spirit directed each.

I began holding casual meetings in the community hall. At first not many came, but after a while the room was filled with all ages. I told stories of my trip to New Hampshire, my book shop, and all the people I met. My audience was intrigued and wanted to learn more about this far-off land. I carefully listened to the Holy Spirit, only speaking what I was directed, realizing too much too soon could frighten some. With His help I was able to be compassionate, loving, and respectful of those who had a deeply imbedded fear rooted in distrust. I knew from experience that change was not easy or always well received.

As Mr. Castleman taught, building trust was the first step to open communication, so I stepped cautiously each time we met. I shared the lessons I had learned about the north, south, east, and west and the instruments that reflected those directions. This seemed to pique their interest, especially the instruments. Holy Spirit quietly spoke to my spirit and said, "This will be a way to communicate and build trust. Go throughout the community and borrow handheld drums, bells, sticks, and rattles." I was amazed how much excitement this created. It even caught some of the teens' attention! By the next meeting there were many new faces. I quietly thanked Abba.

That evening, I began with a talk about oneness, which my people truly understood, for throughout generations they had walked closely with Creator. They understood the need to honor creation, to be one with it, since mankind relied on it to live. Listening to the prompting of the Holy Spirit, I shared about Father God, His Son, and the Holy Spirit, about how though they are separate, they are one. Most people found this extremely difficult to comprehend, but it was well accepted this evening because of my people's unity with Creator, creation, and each other.

Teaching by participation has a lasting effect, as I learned and experienced from Mr. Castleman, and so I continued by explaining what we were about to do. I shared that when a group of people gathered together to play instruments, at first it would be chaotic with no continuous beat; however, as each person listened with their heart, a natural rhythm would evolve and they would all beat as one. I then stated, "This is what it is like to be close to Savior, to be one with Him. It's like we become one heartbeat with Savior Jesus."

As the instruments were passed out, the hesitations and insecurities were bluntly present. As we began, the fear and lack of trust in many eyes saddened me, but Holy Spirit was faithful. As I watched, I witnessed the chaotic beats moving throughout the building into the atmosphere and then slowly evolving into a single beat. I saw walls begin to break down. I witnessed glimmers of joy breaking through my people's beautiful faces.

Bridges of trust began developing, and slowly many began to see and feel the lesson of oneness. It was an exuberant time as we explored the beat of the drum. I encouraged each person to take a turn starting a beat, and all were amazed how each time we would progress into one steady beat.

My people learned they each are important to the whole, that a beat without them is not the same. I added, "This is the way Creator sees

His children." The shyness, hesitation, and insecurities that began the evening in everyone from the elders to the youngsters were gone by the end. It was a great lesson in unity, one mind with Christ, and how a gathering of two or more can move a mountain. I began to see glimmers of hope. Later that evening I wept with joy, for God was truly moving amongst my tribe.

In the following weeks, the lessons continued. One evening I gathered the teens and told them that we were going to make face masks. I suggested they think about how they thought they were perceived by others but told them to make their masks reflections of who they thought they were on the inside. An excitement began to sweep through as they whispered to each other. Secretly, again, I thanked Abba.

The next meeting, we began the face mask meeting by pairing off. Realizing this would be a great lesson in trust and dependency, I watched cautiously as they each selected partners. These teens had experienced so much physically and emotionally, trust was not freely given even amongst each other. With loving encouragement, they eventually paired off.

We began with partners putting Vaseline on each other's face, keeping the eyes and mouth free. They had the option of doing a whole mask or half. I then put strips of paper mache over these beautiful young faces, and everyone lay still on mats at the same time as the masks dried.

I unobtrusively put some Native flute music on my CD player to calm the restlessness in some. All needed to remain still for an hour or so for the paper strips to harden. In the stillness of the room, I spoke about the love of Abba and His Son. I told them how much Creator loved them and that they were not forgotten and never would be. As the masks dried, the peace of Jesus came upon the room. I knew without a doubt that the Holy Spirit led me through this workshop; it was His presence that brought the spirit of reconciliation upon the room.

The excitement began to build in the room as the masks were gently taken off. This was a joy to see. We broke for lunch as the masks dried further, and then I brought out paint, feathers, jewels, beads, and glitter. I was amazed as the teens created masterpieces that depicted who they thought they were. It truly reflected the resilience of a strong people. Some of the most beautiful masks reflected the inner struggles of shame and anger. I was well pleased, for this truly indicated the healing process had begun.

At the next community meeting, the masks were displayed and each participant came to the front to describe his or her creation. The teens proudly showed them to the elders and parents. It was clear that they were empowered through this process and were grateful for being accepted for who they were. The healing continued.

In the following gatherings I talked about recognizing and acknowledging the injustices done to First Nations peoples throughout generations, including the horrendous consequences of Christian missionaries' actions. I shared that without recognition there could be no forgiveness. Some felt they had no reason to forgive and it was just wrong what had happened to them. I understood that and acknowledged their feelings.

I shared that we needed to forgive and overcome not only for our own personal benefit and health but also for the sake of our First Nations. Living in anger and hate was not Creator's way. In addition, I explained, in the future we would need to gather with non-Native people so they could ask for forgiveness, repent, and make amends for the injustices done in order to change the direction their country was headed in. This was God's way of walking in love and forgiveness, for the sake of all involved.

Soon after, the day came when the Holy Spirit said, "Now is the time. Tell them about Savior Jesus this evening." By His grace, earlier that day I had found a Native translation of Hebrews 1:1–3. This was perfection and so I shared the elder's interpretation of this scripture:

Long ago Creator spoke many times and in many ways to our ancestors through prophets. But now in these final days, He has spoken to us through His Son. Creator promised everything to the Son as an inheritance, and through the Son He made the universe and everything in it. The Son reflects the Creator's own glory, and everything about him represents Creator exactly. He sustains the universe by the mighty power of his command. All promises He made to them are fulfilled in Jesus. He is the One who created the world.

He created the water where we go pray in the mornings. He created the fire where we dance and sing. He created the turtles where we get our rattles. He created the smoke that raises up to honor Him. To me it says that any ceremony that is from the Great Spirit will point to Him. If it is true, then it will point to the Truth. He is the fulfillment of the sacred fire, the cleansing fire, the water ceremonies, the sweat lodge and all other things. They all point to Him...

When I pray at water I know He is the One I am thanking. When I dance, I dance to Him. When I bless myself with cedar fire I am realizing that it is His Blood that cleanses me. And when I sweat in the O'si I am thanking Him for a cleansing that never ends.[3]

---

[3] Alexander, Corky. *Native American Pentecost* (Cleveland, TN: Cherohala Press, 2012), 149-150.

A hush had fallen over the room. I continued by saying, "This is the true Son of God, Jesus the Christ, the one who will save and guide us through all things in life. This is the same Savior that our elders were taught about by missionaries; however, the missionaries sadly missed sharing the true heart of Savior, which is unconditional love and acceptance.

"A great heartbreak occurred in us when truth was corrupted by man's ego. His interpretations of the Bible became religious, filled with rules and dogmas that became more important than following the Word of God. Missionaries did not accept us unconditionally. They did not teach that walking the Jesus path in life, honoring God Creator, and living with the guidance of the Holy Spirit is the only way to a peaceful life.

"There is healing through Jesus. You can overcome, for there is forgiveness and reconciliation through Jesus. He is the way, the truth, and the life." I then shared my story of when I accepted Yahshua into my life and called those forward who also wanted this free gift. Holy Spirit moved mightily. The room was filled as my brothers and sisters came forward. We hugged and wept. The love that enveloped the room was undeniable, and for many of my people, it was the first time they felt loved.

Chapter 6

The Ultimate Gift of Forgiveness

WHEN ONE MENTIONS FORGIVENESS, DEFENSES immediately arise. Why should I forgive? What good would it do me? It was their fault, and therefore they need to apologize to me. And the comments can go on and on.

History has shown us that my people experienced horrific demoralization at the hand of those who attempted to destroy their culture. What other people throughout history have had to endure such atrocities? When considering this, one immediately thinks of the Jewish people, the Holocaust and Hitler, but the world was behind them . . . a war was fought and the people were set free.

This was not the case with First Nations people; no one came to our aid. We were a people that existed peacefully on the land before "white man" arrived. We have not been provided proper restitutions and have not had our land restored. Apologies have not been proclaimed.

71

Why were my people stripped of their identity and left to inhumane conditions on reservations for the sake of government, the wealth of others, and the expansion of Christianity?

The anger runs deep. Before my trip home, I found this poem, "Thanksgiving Poem," written by Jonathan Garfield. A few lines say it all:

> *Thank you for relocating relations, relocating their hearts, some forgetting or ashamed of their Indigenous roots.*
>
> *Thank you for Catholic boarding school surgeons painfully removing our Native tongue without anesthetic until our mouths bled English.*
>
> *Thank you for the children starving reservations wide, left alone and staying up late, hoping their parent or parents didn't drink or shoot up all the check.*
>
> *Thank you for the reservation suicides that have killed the spirits of those left behind.[4]*

Unforgiveness keeps us in bondage. It tortures our souls and leads to anger in every area of life. It controls, destroys, and creates divisions. It separates families, pushes people to violence, and causes wars, hate crimes, addictions, cancer, autoimmune diseases, depression, and so much more. It prevents us from living the life God intended for His children and blocks blessings.

---

[4] Website – Indian Country Today Media Network https://newsmaven.io/indiancountrytoday/archive/thanksgiving-a-poem-by-jonathan-garfield-hHK2ksuqskKKLO8spK8SSw/ Garfield, Jonathan. November 28, 2013.

I was once consumed with a lethal spirit of unforgiveness and anger and would say, "My anger is justified." I refused to move from this state. I had to look deep within and ask, is this truly the way to live? Do I want to be consumed with hate, pain, strife, and unforgiveness? Living this way was certainly not walking the Jesus way in life! Even on the cross Jesus prayed, "Father, forgive them for they know not what they do" (Luke 23:34).

As a believer, I needed to make a drastic change. This became one of the hardest lessons yet. I realized if Jesus could forgive those who crucified Him, I too must forgive all the past injustices done to me and my people. This was the second ultimate gift from Savior that changed my life—forgiveness.

Mr. Castleman taught that strife is truly not the walk of a follower of Jesus. He said, "Discontentment is a dangerous place to live." He asked, "Do you really want to poison your life daily with unforgiveness, angry thoughts and words?" He then shared that God wants us to pray for our enemies. Matthew 5:44 says,

"But I say unto you, love your enemies, bless those who curse you, do good to those who hate you, and pray for those who spitefully use you and persecute you."

Immediately I stated, "This is so unfair. They don't deserve my prayers." Mr. Castleman said, "That is not the point. God says pray for them. Forgiveness is for your sake, not the sake of the offender. By forgiving you will move yourself to a place of blessing, favor in Creator's eyes." He then continued teaching by stating, "That is being a believer in Savior. We are not to walk by the flesh or feelings; this new way of living is to be a life of faith."

It was not easy. In fact, it was a gut-wrenching challenge at times. But God said to pray, so I did. God said bless my enemies, not to curse them or speak evil of them, and slowly I did. Over time this moved me to new levels of love and compassion. The times my flesh was winning and I still felt anger over the injustices, I would cry out to Abba and He helped me with my hardened heart. Eventually, Jesus provided the way for me to overcome and begin to release my anger and heal my soul.

My thinking was gradually changing; my mind was being renewed with Mr. Castleman's teachings. Daily spending time reading and meditating in the Word, I was slowly moving from living a carnal life to living a spirit-led one, which in turn began to heal my soul and help me move past unresolved anger issues. I am so grateful to Savior and this healing path; however, I remained perplexed as to how I could relay this ultimate gift of forgiveness to my people. I prayed and quietly asked the Holy Spirit for guidance.

Chapter 7

A Stranger In Town

MR. CASTLEMAN'S TEACHINGS, I REALIZE NOW were always taught in God's timing. All that he imparted prepared me to teach my brothers and sisters these next lessons. I shared that man is made of a body, soul, and spirit, that we are triune beings just like God is. Creator God functions as a Father, He functions as a Son, and He functions as Holy Spirit, our great comforter. We are a reflection of Him!

Mr. Castleman said the Bible, also known as the Word, would set me free. He said it contains "dunamis power"—miracle performing power that can change lives. It is a guide on how we should live daily. It can heal the body, emotions, and spirit if you spend time absorbing the Word until it is more real on the inside than what you see in the natural.

I was taught that either you are walking in the God kind of love or you are walking in fear. The Word teaches that perfect love casts out all fear. In love, there is no fear; therefore, when fear arose in my life, I was to look at what I was thinking, what was I judging, and where my focus was. All fears and worries must be captured and replaced by the Word which is truth.

All these lessons were remarkable and life-changing, but truthfully, it was not an easy journey. I remember when I was so distraught, crying at the river, lying on the cool, damp ground and I heard the Lord say to me, "You have a choice: stay here and wallow in your past or get up, release the pain, and move on." Holy Spirit quietly whispered, "This is where you begin with your people. Help them release their pain. Let Savior be the example."

Our weekly gatherings continued, and I saw a community of people coming together step by step. By the leading of the Lord, I began Sunday worship gatherings. We sang and danced unto the Lord in our regalia, with our instruments and dark-colored skin. We were loved and accepted unconditionally by Savior and each other. Brothers and sisters were becoming more confident in their walks with Jesus and would share testimonies of Creator working in their lives. I was blessed and well pleased.

One afternoon there was talk of a stranger in town near the Rez. My people were always hesitant to allow anyone on or near the Rez. Undoubtedly this was a result of the past. I, on the other hand, became intrigued and took a trip into the nearby town. It did not take long to find this mysterious person because the Holy Spirit directed my every step, which initially puzzled me . . . until I saw who it was sitting at the café table.

My heart leaped with joy! I was overwhelmed with emotions as I ran into the arms of my dear mentor, Mr. Bob Castleman. "How? Why? Here?" I blathered with tears streaming down my face. I was speechless and overcome with emotions. With the calming presence of peace and love that always exuded from Mr. Castleman, I was able to compose myself and at his request sat at his table.

Catching up with old friends is a blessing, but this meeting was beyond words. Mr. Castleman was always about Father God's work, and without hesitation, he began speaking. He daily prayed for all his students and at times Holy Spirit would give him revelations when one was in need of help. Looking at me with eyes of love and light, he said, "So tell me, how have you been and what do you need help with?"

I talked all about my journey thus far and the need to help my people move to forgiveness, for their own sake. Mr. Castleman was delighted with all that I shared and looked like a proud papa sitting there, which made me smile inside. He said I had done well with what knowledge I had so far and he was there to help me and my people move to walking the Jesus way in life fully.

He then asked if it would be possible for him to stay on the Rez for a while. However, not wanting to impose or make anyone uncomfortable, he added that whatever the answer was, we could work with it.

That evening at the community meeting, I shared that my dear friend Mr. Castleman was in town. They knew of him because of all the stories I had shared, and to my surprise, they said he could stay as long as he needed. A brother came forward and insisted he bunk with him. I thanked God for the openness and trust seeds that had been planted, for that evening I saw fruit.

Mr. Castleman fit right in immediately, and I was grateful. Truthfully I had no doubts. He joined our weekly meetings and attended Sunday worship, at first just watching, then doing what he was most gifted at, teaching thirsty believers. Our first lesson was about judgment. He said there are a few words we need to avoid using that will help keep us from making judgments:

1. I judge if I . . . worry. Worry judges God; it says He can't handle things in your life. Worry edges God out,

which is another way of saying your ego is in control, not God. Prayer and worship carry worries away.

2. I judge if I . . . have expectations of others. We are to give freely, whether it is our love, time, gifts, or talents, and not expect anything in return. If there is an expectation, then there is a judgment and control attached. Jesus the Christ is a perfect example of giving freely.

3. I judge if I . . . have my own agenda. Daily we need to be living according to God's agenda, not our own.

4. I judge if I . . . set limitations on myself or other people. If you have a need to know or control things and other people, then you are setting limitations and not allowing God to do what He knows is best for you and the situation.

5. I judge if I . . . use these terms in thought or spoken word: *what if, if only, can't, should, and try or trying.* Think about your own words. How often do you say, "If only I could" or any of its variations? How many times have you "shoulded" yourself or others? These are not uplifting, encouraging, inspiring phrases; they all speak defeat before the process even begins!

6. I judge if I . . . feel the need to defend myself. The root cause of defensiveness is personal insecurity based on beliefs from childhood teachings, people and things

that molded your life. Your belief in yourself needs to be based on the Word of God and who you are in Christ. If you are born of Christ, He lives in you!

7. I judge if I . . . rationalize my behavior. Rationalizing is the same as defending yourself. You are made in the image of God. Study God and His attributes in the Bible and begin to apply them to your life. You will become confident and no longer feel the need to defend and explain.

8. I judge if I . . . label things. We are a society that labels everything, which ultimately results in judgment. Start looking at life through Jesus' eyes and your outlook will completely change to one of compassion for yourself and others. All labels will disappear, and love will remain.

9. I judge if I . . . gossip. Gossips repeat details about another person's life which can result in judgments, harm, jealousy, and contempt. Nothing good can come from gossip. God is the only one that truly knows a person and his/her heart.

Mr. Castleman said that judgments are limiting and the greatest cause of illness. They create hate, and when hate festers inside your body, illness will surely come, whether it is physical sickness or a mental addiction. Judgments will keep you focused on the wrong thoughts, create havoc in your life, and prevent you from hearing from God.

He continued by teaching us about words, about how we speak

creates our future. He said, "If you don't like where you are in life today, then change your thoughts, which will change your words, which will change your life. Words are seeds, and they can produce fruit. What you focus on will produce more of the same outcome. For example, when a child is misbehaving, change your dance step. Instead of focusing on the negative behavior, replace your response to something that he or she can learn and grow from." Mr. Castleman then added we just need to be creative in situations instead of reactive. He said, "Simply move the C in the word reactive and be creative instead."

That evening he ended the lesson by teaching on Philippians 4:8–9:

> Finally, brethren, whatsoever things are true, whatsoever things are honest, whatsoever things are just, whatsoever things are pure, whatsoever things are lovely, whatsoever things are of good report; if there be any virtue, and if there be any praise, think on these things. Those things which ye have both learned, and received, and heard, and seen in me, do: and the God of peace shall be with you.

Chapter 8

Reconciliation

MR. CASTLEMAN'S LESSONS CONTINUED, AND I could feel the peace of Yahshua resting upon the Rez, bringing a new hope and restoration. My people were thirsty and in awe of this new nonjudgmental teaching of Creator's Son. They were taught that the Word says we are all equipped with spiritual gifts, all are needed and loved.

Every person who walks the Jesus way has a gifting, and depending on their calling, more than one. All believers of Jesus have a calling and purpose in life, not just pastors or ministers, as organized religion teaches. Mr. Castleman said, "There are people in your life who will see your words and actions. As you walk the Jesus way in life, lives will be changed, including yours. Through this type of living you will bring hope to your tribe and surrounding communities."

Mr. Castleman continued by saying, "Brothers and sisters, this is a process that we must be patient with." As in the past, he was always visual with his teachings. We were all excited when he announced we were making soap. "Soap making," he said, "is a process. Much like all things in this life, it takes patience, perseverance, and more patience."

Our soap making class was wonderful and filled with many lessons. As Mr. Castleman moved through the soap making steps, he talked about the connection built through each step so that the end result would be accomplished. In life, as we walk the Jesus way, the end result is to love one another with compassion and a lot of patience. Mr. Castleman said, "Through this type of intent living, connections and relationships are formed with each step taken, and then we truly live as God intended, helping each other in all things."

Then he said, it was time that we break down the walls between Christian religions, between saved and unsaved people, between Native and white; between the labels put on everyone and everything and focus on the one, Yahshua. Jesus Christ is our example of pure love, forgiveness, and reconciliation, and this is the walk we need to emulate.

Mr. Castleman was excited to share that today there was a great movement that had begun with the goal of reconciliation. He said, "There are many who have realized the injustices done to you and want to gather and apologize. However, for that to happen you have to lean on the love of Savior inside to be compassionate and open to receiving them.

"You are not alone, for Jesus said He would send a helper, a comforter to help you with your walk on this earth, and His name is Holy Spirit. He is our comforter, our guide, our small, quiet voice that is willing to teach and help us through every moment in life. He will guide your every step; He will comfort you in your pain and help you release deep wounds. With His help, you will be open to let white man step onto your reservation to ask for forgiveness."

Mr. Castleman taught that we must all understand that reconciliation is an instrumental part of healing and restoration in the human race.

We can move from past hurts if we follow the teachings of the greatest example that walked on this earth, Yahshua. We can overcome. Jesus reconciled us to Creator God when man fell short; we can do this too with mankind as we walk by faith.

Pure, honest communication is critical and fundamental for reaching a hurt individual, no less a nation of people, no matter creed or race. It is important to build relationships and talk about the past in order to move beyond it. It will be the grace and mercy of God along with the healing presence of the Holy Spirit that will allow all people of the world to heal.

When there is true reconciliation, there will be a confession of sin to God or others who have been offended, there will be forgiveness and establishment of new relationships, and there will be peace. However, this will not happen overnight. It will be a progression of humble steps over time with all parties involved. Mr. Castleman ended the evening asking the crucial question: were we ready to forgive? Were we ready to receive people outside our Rez who wanted to ask for forgiveness?

To my surprise, without hesitation my brothers and sisters responded openly, "Yes, we are ready." This truly was the movement of the Holy Spirit. Never in my lifetime would I have imagined this would be possible. At that point, Mr. Castleman explained that he knew a group of people he had been working with who truly wanted to move toward healing for the sake of First Nations people and our nation.

The following weeks were filled with anticipation and a bit of anxiety. We held numerous prayer meetings knowing that Creator God heard our prayers. We reached out to other tribes and called for a powwow of reconciliation.

Our Native powwow represents the circle of life; it's a gathering of relatives of all ages. It is people reconnecting with old friends and a time when children learn the traditions of their culture. The day of the powwow, we all dressed in our ceremonial regalia to honor Creator God and our guests. We began the grand entry procession with leaders carrying numerous flags representing different tribes. They were followed by veterans who had fought in our wars, then elders, adults, and finally children.

Our honored guests were welcomed as we continued with the beat of the drum and dancing. We shared that for First Nations people, the beat of the drum represents the beat of the heart. The powwow always reminds us who we are and renews our spirit, and it is through the beat and dance that we get reconnected.

In perfect time, Mr. Castleman proceeded with a ceremony of reconciliation. Our guests gave us a gift, and we reciprocated according to our tradition. Then their representative spoke of the shame and guilt their ancestors had brought upon their lives with the injustices done to a beautiful people, apologized, and asked for forgiveness.

I held my breath as my tribe leader stood before them, wondering what would happen. She then spoke of Yahshua and walking His way in life and graciously accepted their apology. Our guests then presented us with a stone from a piece of land that had been illegally acquired decades ago which they were now deeding back to us. I was witnessing miraculous healing throughout my people. Tears were flowing through smiles of hope, something I had never seen nor will I ever forget. I thanked my God for His hand, for His grace and mercy upon us and our guests.

As the powwow ended and our guests left, I eagerly looked for Mr. Castleman to thank him for his help. I couldn't find him anywhere. But instead of panicking like the last time he left, this time I smiled and reveled in the peace I felt. Holy Spirit assured me that our paths would cross again someday.

I saw a renewed hope and excitement over the next weeks and

months amongst my people. They began to confidently reach out beyond the Rez. They worked with non-Natives and began to change their poor living conditions. The Rez finally had clean water and proper electricity. I was humbled, amazed, and blessed by the work Yahuwah had done over the year. I knew we were on the road to great healing for my people and the nation.

For me personally, it was time to move on to the next chapter in my life, though I wasn't sure what that would be. One thing I did know was life is an adventure and a series of journeys. We always have a choice as to which direction we want to take—a path toward hate and strife or a journey to peace, love, and forgiveness.

As I sat waiting on the Lord, I heard Yahuwah directing me to be still. In my spirit I heard, "Dwell in the secret place of the most high" (Psalm 91). I was moved to tears, as I fondly remembered this was the very first scripture that I read with Mr. Castleman. It seemed so long ago, yet the time was fleeting. I thanked God for His faithful servant Mr. Castleman, for the love of Jesus and the miraculous healings and breakthroughs.

Father God then instructed I needed to spend time at a retreat in the mountains to prepare for my next journey. As I communed with Creator God and waited on His directions, I experienced a deeper healing to my body, soul, and spirit and a new level of intimacy. I praised Him with hands lifted in gratitude and thanksgiving. I worshipped Him with my drum, rattles, bells, and dance without hesitation as who He created me to be.

God, the creator of the universe, loves me! I have purpose in my life because of the love of a Savior, Jesus Christ. I am humbled and ever so grateful. I now can love and forgive with the compassion of Jesus. I am now able to show the world how to live and walk the Jesus way, always giving God the glory now and forever.

I am now ready to begin my next journey to peace wherever He will take me, and what a journey that will be! My name is Shawana. I am blessed and forever God's faithful loving daughter . . .

God's blessings and peace ~

Chapter 9

Epilogue – A Great Awakening

BILLY GRAHAM ONCE REFERRED TO THE FIRST Nations people as a "sleeping giant." As I was writing this parable, Mr. Graham went to be with the Lord. He was a great man of God who touched many lives, and his work lives on today. I see his prophetic words coming to pass, as a great awakening has begun amongst the First Nations people and non-Native people alike.

Many Native believers are reaching their fellow brothers and sisters. They are encouraging them, helping people heal, breaking down walls and spreading the truth about Yahshua and His love for all mankind. On my website, www.journeystopeace.com, I have a list of some of these trail blazers and their websites/social media pages. If led by the Lord, please support them to help heal First Nations people and our nation. We can change and heal. We can move from bitterness to love and overcome the Jesus way.

As I close, I want to share with you this love letter I received for First Nations people. It tells them about Jesus Christ, the Way Maker, the one who will heal a nation of people and bring about a great revival amongst the ones who first occupied the land:

My dearest ones, all of you among the tribes of First Nations people that occupied these lands, hear My voice. You have known Me as Creator, walked with Me, learned My ways, and protected My land. The land provided and nourished you. I showed you food to eat, herbs that heal, and warmth. The water was pure and the earth was green and lush. It is not so today.

There is a great need for revival across this nation, for the land, water, and people. It is those who caused great harm to you that now need help, and I am calling upon you as First Nations people to heed the call. For it is only you who know the dire deplorable state of the earth. You have been beaten, abused, moved from land to land until there was not much left for you. We still walk together, but chasms of all the incomprehensible atrocities, plights, and deep hurts have come between us at the hand of the evil one.

I am asking that you come to intimately know the One who will help you move through your pain and the injustices of the past. That is my Son, Jesus the Christ. For you see, as you come to know Him, you will see the way, the truth, and the life. He is Savior.

White man under the name of Christianity has stolen you from My arms. They have told you lies and deceived many great tribal leaders and your people for their own gain. I have seen what they did in the name of Christianity. It continues today and saddens Me greatly.

There is an awakening of many of you realizing the truth and moving away from the abuse from the past. This awakening can only be done with my Son by walking the Jesus way. In Him there is love, compassion, and forgiveness. With Him you will be able to stand tall, embrace your heritage, and your culture, and walk the way I originally intended, with Me, My Son, and the Holy Spirit without judgment.

It is time to move beyond the past and the present, to look to what is coming: a great revival stemming from a great people. You are needed. Your warriors are needed to awaken people across the land with their drums, dance, and worship unto Me. You may have felt as if you were alone, but I have never left you. It is only lies of the evil one and the people he used with the spirit of greed that are keeping you from Me.

You have a choice. You are not victims, helpless, desolate, and alone. My Son is waiting for you to come to Him as you are, with your regalia, drums, dance, smudging, and sweat lodges. You know what it is like to walk closely with Me. A newfound freedom can be found with my Son.

It is My Son, Jesus the Christ, who heals, mends the broken hearted, and brings joy and peace that surpasses all understanding. It is only through Him, the Way Maker, that you will break free from the bondages of the past.

I need you! The governments, the people of the United States, have made choices that will bring disastrous consequences upon them. It is you, My chosen First Nations people of this great land, who will bring revival. The people of America are lost in their Christianity, denominations, rules, and judgments. The people are lost in their cultures and immoralities. Desecrations to My Word will bring great judgment upon this land. It was never meant to be this way. If people walked with My Son and stayed true to My Holy Word, none of this would be.

Arise First Nations people; arise and take your stand. Those who others think are the lowly I will use for My greater purpose. You are born for a time such as this! Listen to your brothers and sisters amongst your people who are already spreading the good news of the Jesus way. Know the Way Maker will lead you.

A great shift is coming, and you will be the center of it. You need to lead a call to repentance on behalf of this nation. I will hear you in the heavens if you do this, for it is you who have been in bondage and captivity as My children in Egypt were.

"Now, therefore," says the Lord,
"Turn to Me with all your heart,
With fasting, weeping and mourning.
So rend your heart, and not your garments;
Return to the Lord your God,
For He is gracious and merciful,
Slow to anger and of great kindness;
And He relents from doing harm." Joel 2:12–13

Only with your belief in My Son will your cries be heard. Release the past, step into your future calling, and walk with My Son Jesus. Repent from your sins, anger, hurts, judgments, addictions, abuse, generational curses, anything that would jeopardize your relationship with Me. Forgive, forgive, forgive as My Son did. Jesus the Christ takes all sins, past, present, and future and His blood covers all of them. Trust in Him and move into your calling. He is your Savior!

The time is short. You are needed now. Hear My call. May your powwows be of worship to Me. May your drums beat out to the nations and tribes of this great calling. May your dancing and song be of thanksgiving to My Son, and I will embrace you as My sons and daughters; I will be your Father Abba and welcome you into my Kingdom just as you are.

Be still and know that I am your God. I am Creator whom you have known all along. I long for you. I love you my First Nations people.

Will you take your place so the humbled will be exalted? Will you stand with the Way Maker, Jesus the Christ, so man will see what they are doing to the land called America? For it will no longer be tolerated!

You are My people, My First Nations people who honored Me and the land from the beginning.

Beat the drum. Call out to all First Nations people, the warriors of peace. Follow My Son, Jesus the Christ, the Way Maker, and He will show you a great and mighty works with miracles and healings across that which was once a great land!

Revival will break out. My people will come back to Me. Nations will be restored, all that has been stolen by the evil one will be returned, and peace could settle upon America until My Son returns. The choice is yours.

Bibliography

"100 Years; One Woman's Fight For Justice" – Documentary
https://www.netflix.com/title/80144983

Alexander, Corky. *Native American Pentecost – Praxis, Contextualization, Transformation.* Cleveland, TN: Cherohala Press, 2012.

Hayford, Jack W. *The New Spirit Filled Bible, NKJ,* Nashville, TN: Thomas Nelson, Inc., 2002.

Indian Country Today Media Network,
https://newsmaven.io/indiancountrytoday/archive/thanksgiving-a-poem-by-jonathan-garfield-hHK2ksuqskKKLO8spK8SSw/

Wilson, James. The Earth Shall Weep. New York, NY: Grove Press, 1999.

Afterward

Journeys to Peace was created from a blending of personal experiences and facts originally adapted for my master's thesis on the *First Nations People Past, Present and Future*. The thesis captured the true historical facts of Native American people and the injustices they experienced in the past and continue to endure today.

Witnessing how deeply moved my professor was reading the thesis, being part Native herself, I was intrigued at the thought of publishing the paper as she suggested but recognized it was not an enjoyable read in its current state. Through prayer and waiting on the Lord, *Journeys to Peace* was planted in my heart with the desire to tell this God-inspired story so healing could begin for all people, especially First Nations people.

Through the help of the Holy Spirit, *Journeys to Peace* was written as a parable to teach about the love of a Savior and the power of forgiveness. It incorporates many personal life lessons taught to me by a special person in my life—lessons on the four directions, drum circles, making a drum, face masks, soap, judgments, and so much more. Some were great fun, others challenging and life-changing. Nevertheless, all were powerful teaching tools.

Through my special friend, I was introduced to people from the Oneida Indian Nation Tribe and personally witnessed the heartache that still keeps them and their Native brothers and sisters in bondage today. In this book I've shared some of these experiences while incorporating historical facts with the intent that people would move to love and forgiveness personally and collectively as a nation.

I pray this parable touched your soul and brought you to a place of peace knowing that you are loved by Creator God; His Son, Jesus Christ; and the Holy Spirit. You are unique, you are needed, and you have a purpose to fulfill in life. I pray all your journeys are journeys to peace.

God's blessings and peace ~

TR

Let All Things Praise Him

Praise God in His sanctuary;
Praise Him in His mighty firmament!

Praise Him for His mighty acts;
Praise Him according to His excellent greatness!

Praise Him with the sound of the trumpet;
Praise Him with the lute and harp!
Praise Him with the timbrel and dance;
Praise Him with stringed instruments and flutes!
Praise Him with loud cymbals;
Praise Him with clashing cymbals!

Let everything that has breath praise the LORD.

Praise the LORD!
Psalm 150

CPSIA information can be obtained
at www.ICGtesting.com
Printed in the USA
BVHW030856290419
546813BV00007B/24/P

9 781973 656425